DRAW IT!
COLOUR IT!
CREATURES

MACMILLAN CHILDREN'S BOOKS

Go on, add some teeth.
I dare you!

Axel Scheffler

HAMISH THE

Hairy Dog

(just add hair)

Emily Gravett

MY
RARE BUTTERFLY
COLLECTION

RARE BUTTERFLY no.1

RARE BUTTERFLY no.2

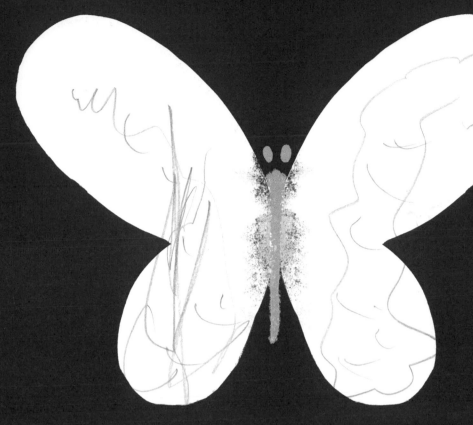

RARE BUTTERFLY no.3

Four of the
most unusual
butterflies in
the world.

YOU
can make
it happen!

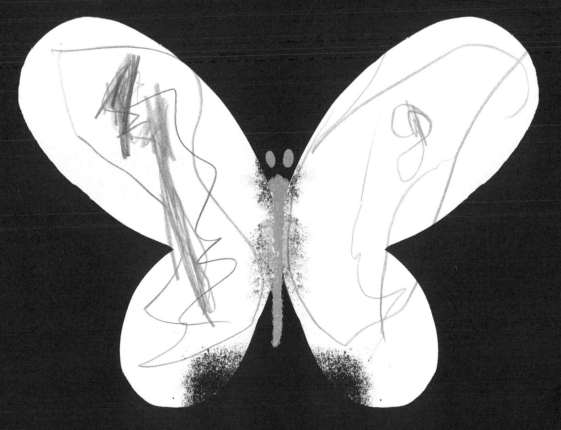

RARE BUTTERFLY no.4

tjmhopgood

Find all 6 fish and
colour them in!

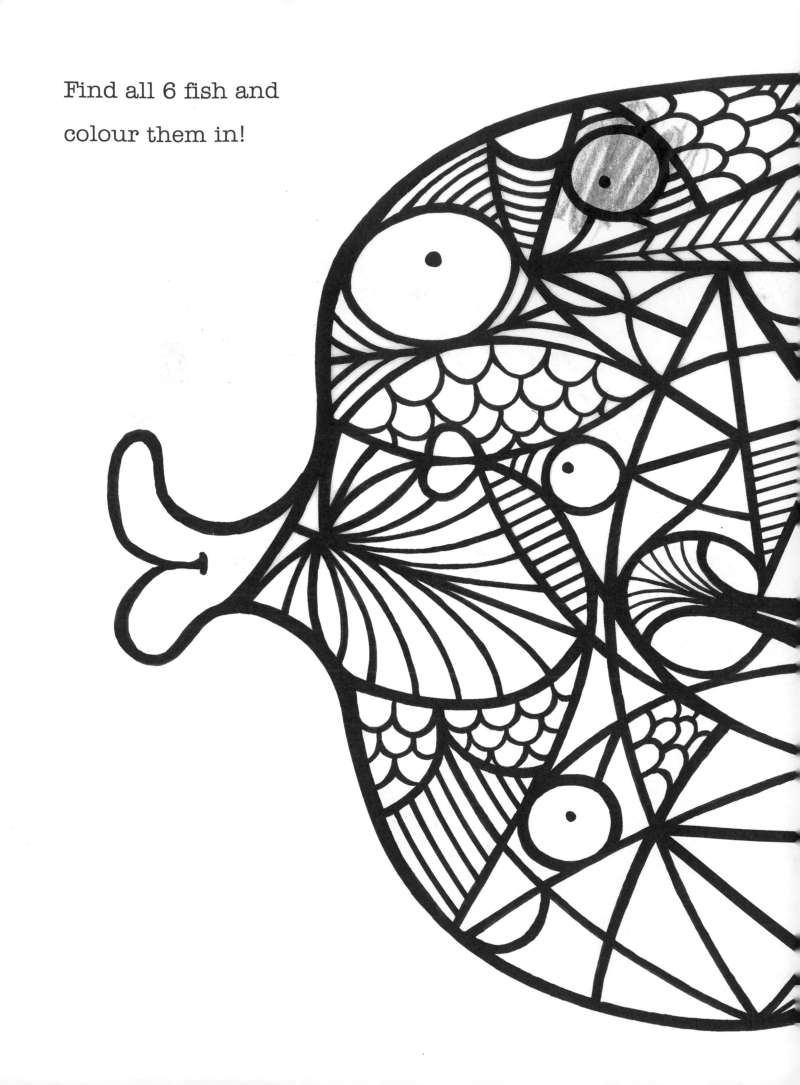

Matt Spink

Squirrel wears a wig.

Duck wears a hat.

What will you draw for Penguin and Cat?

An armchair, a bike and a very old telly.

What else has this hungry whale got in her belly?

Rob Biddulph

Bear can't leave until the train is full!

Can you help him fill each carriage?

BiRGiTTA SiF

Draw their dreams...

Heavy snowstorm! Draw the penguins in caps and scarves! Add extra penguins too, for warmth!

Susanne Göhlich

This little beast is having a feast!

Can you draw his picnic?

Draw his picnic pal!

Sara Ogilvie

Draw the dragon's fiery flames...

Draw the other monster in the monster battle!

Alexis Deacon

Who's making all that noise?

YOU decide.

DRAW
WHO LIVES
IN THE
HOUSE

DRAW
WHO
DRIVES
THESE CARS

EKATERINA
TRUKHAN

Can you draw the other half, to make a full creature?

Tor Freeman

HUNGRY BUGS AND INSECTS

are eating
all my plants...

Leave
some
for
me!

David Mackintosh

What's the pigeon looking at?

Give him some friends and

fill the tree with golden leaves.

JIM FIELD

DRAW the weirdest creature
you have EVER seen

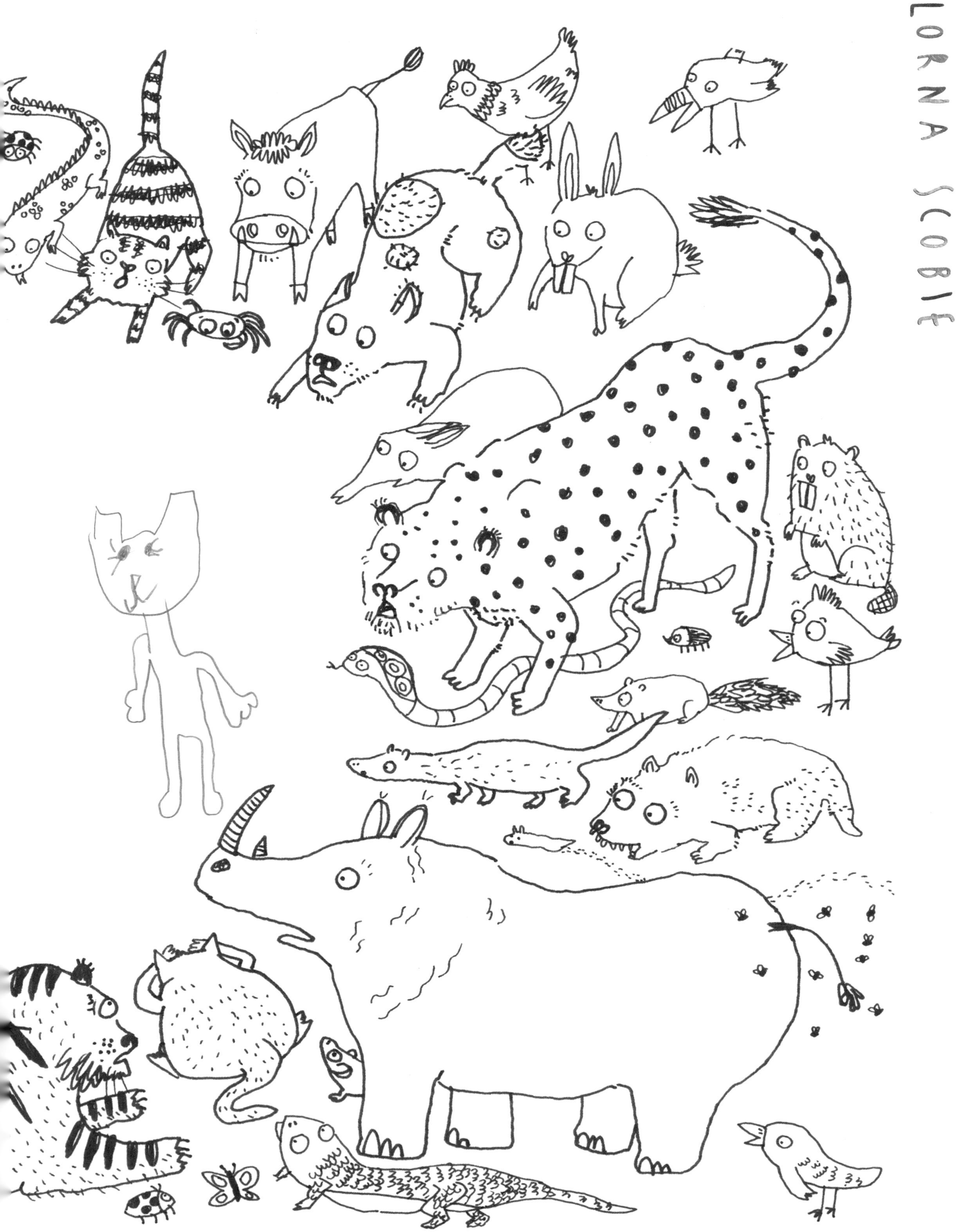
LORNA SCOBIE

Will someone join me for a drink?

Benjamin Chaud

WHAT OTHER
CREATURES
LIVE IN THE
TREE?

Briony May Smith

Oh no! He's being eaten alive! But what by?

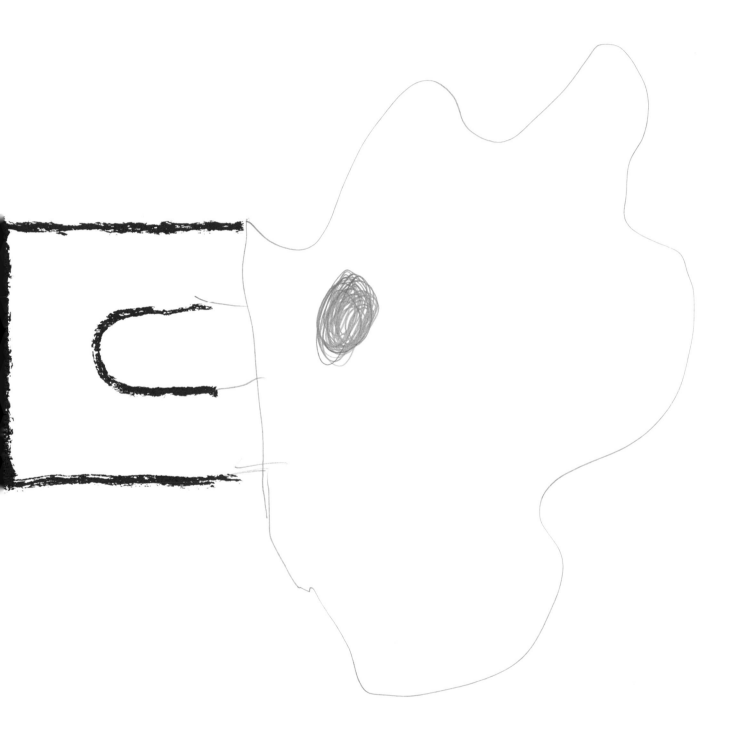

Jean Jullien

Can you help and make

the sheep woolly and warm?

Britta Teckentrup

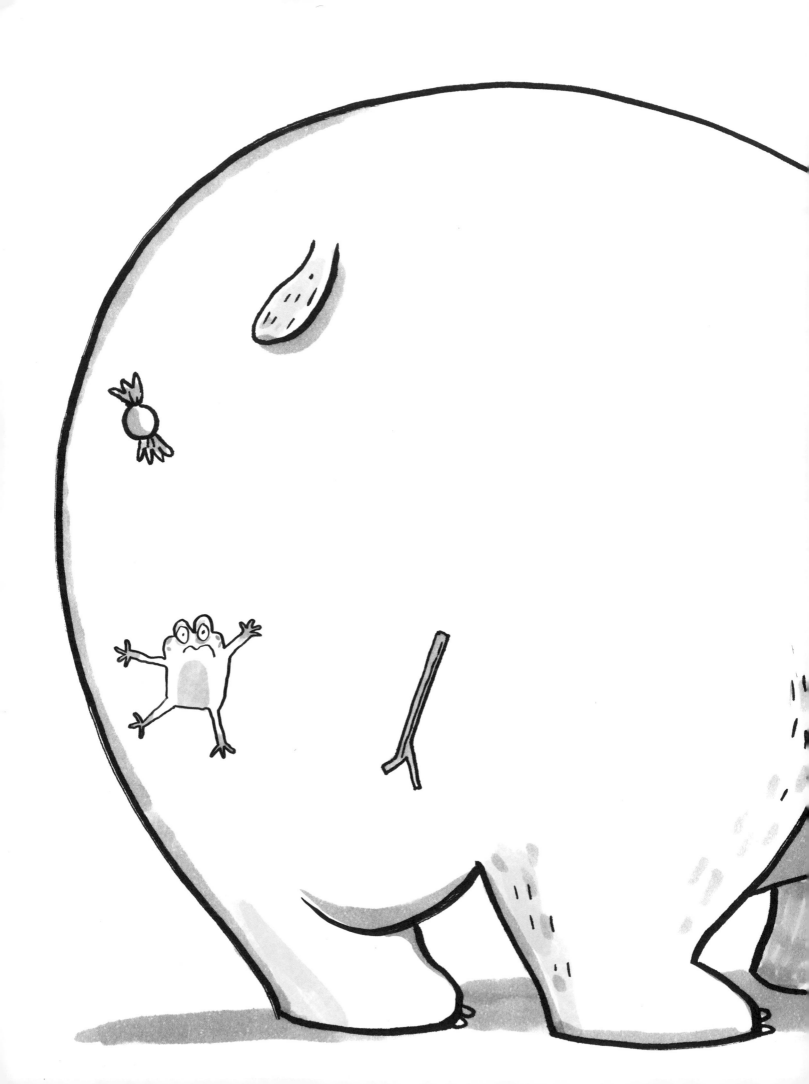

DRAW WHAT'S STUCK TO BEAR'S BUM!

Nikki Dyson.

What does the Baby Alien's Spaceship look like?!

Rebecca
Patterson

What a lot of rubbish! Can you transform
this rubbish into fun creatures?

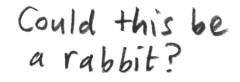

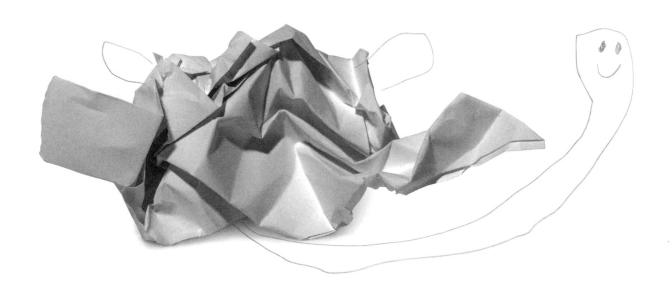

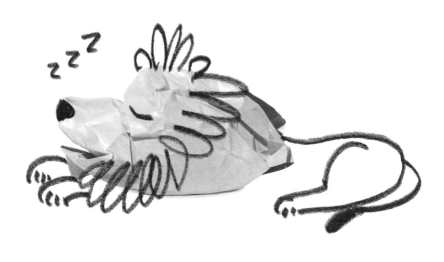

A monster?

Have fun!

Zehra Hicks

Make this a dog.

Make this a cat.

Yasmeen Ismail

Who is this bear hugging?

The three-headed beast is missing two heads!

Can you help?

BARBARA NASCIMBENI

Whose shoes?

Can you draw the rest?

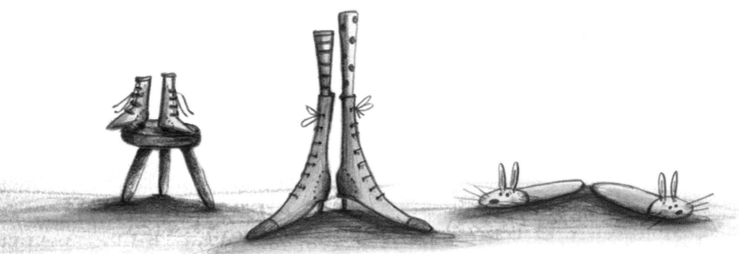

TWO
MONSTERS
(or possibly more . . .)

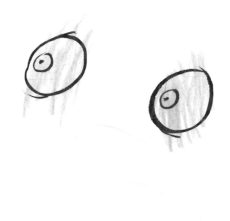

Chris Riddell

DRAW MORE FISH FOR THIS MERMAID TO PHOTOGRAPH.

marta altés

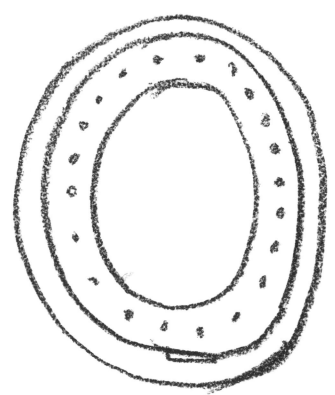

My Deer Mother

MEET MY FAMILY
and OTHER CREATURES

Headmaster

Cousin Ying

Cousin Yang

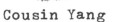

David Mackintosh

Half Brother Mike

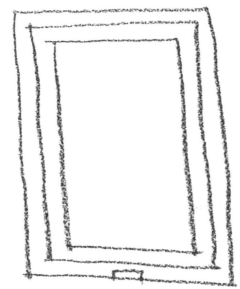

Uncle Xark

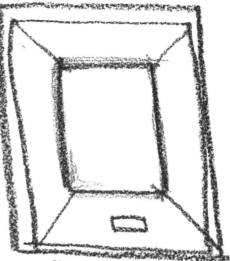

My Sister Pearl

Grandma Jeremy

Cousin
Bradley

Dear Father

Captain Sergeant,

My Nanny

Auntie Penny

Aunt Melanie

Little Minky

My First Pet,
Martin

Colour me in, please.

(Can you make my tail wag too?)

Uh oh, this painter is NOT paying attention and this lady is furious! She's covered in paint! Can you draw her?

JIM FIELD

They're all VERY hungry...

But what will

they eat?

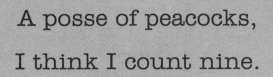
A posse of peacocks,
I think I count nine.

Brighten each tail
with its own
cool design.

Rob Biddulph

What does this airship look like?

Kazuno Kohara

SARAH McINTYRE SHOWS YOU HOW TO DRAW A BIRD...

WITH A REAL FEATHER!

A SMALL ROBIN FEATHER WILL GIVE YOU A VERY DIFFERENT LINE TO A HUGE SWAN OR SEAGULL FEATHER! STAY ON THE LOOKOUT FOR FEATHERS YOU CAN USE!

YOU WILL NEED: A FEATHER
A SHARP KNIFE & <u>AN ADULT</u> TO HELP CUT
A SURFACE TO CUT ON (LIKE A KITCHEN BOARD)
INK (ANY COLOUR)
PAPER (YOU CAN STAIN IT WITH TEA IF YOU WANT TO MAKE IT LOOK OLD!)
KITCHEN ROLL (FOR MESS & BLOTTING YOUR NIB)

LAY FEATHER ON A CUTTING BOARD

CUT OFF TIP AT A SHARP ANGLE

NOW YOU HAVE A POINTY NIB!

DIP ONLY THE TIP!

INK

IF YOUR NIB BREAKS OR DULLS, JUST CUT IT FURTHER UP THE SHAFT OF THE FEATHER!

HERE'S ONE WAY TO DRAW A BIRD WITH YOUR QUILL PEN:

NOW YOU TRY.

CAT

↓

DOG

↓

MOUSE

↓

Russell dyto

Can you draw Cat's space rocket?

Natalie Russell

Spots or stripes?

You decide!

Britta Teckentrup

This floor looks very empty! Shall we fill it up?

What do you think is happening on this floor?

Give him a lady

Sven Nordqvist

COLOUR THE BUGS!

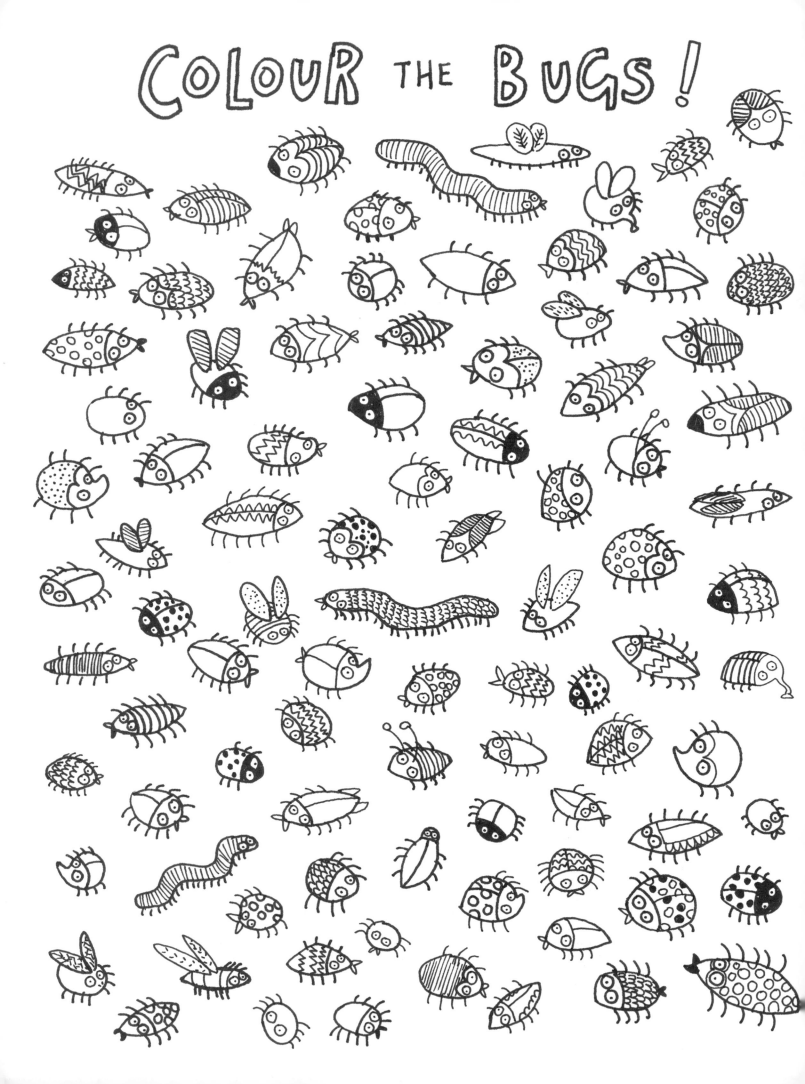

LORNA SCOBIE

Adam Stower

Granny has an interesting new pet. What is it?

Gosh! That's a snazzy cardigan!

Who, or what, is wearing it?

Alex T. Smith

Make me a

colourful cat!

Matt Spink

Can you draw his dancing buddy?

Sara Ogilvie

Draw the creatures that live in these houses...

Alexis Deacon

Draw the birds!

Sven Nordqvist

The Teddy Bears' Picnic!

Can you draw some food in the bears' bellies,
some leaves on the trees, owls in the hollows,
spots on the toadstools and flowers on the stalks?

Emily Mackenzie

It's the Monster Ball tonight.

These customers would like a fancy hair-do!

Jools Bentley

Colour in these creatures.

Now turn these shapes into something fun!

Benji Davies

Poor Stephen! What has

he been eating?

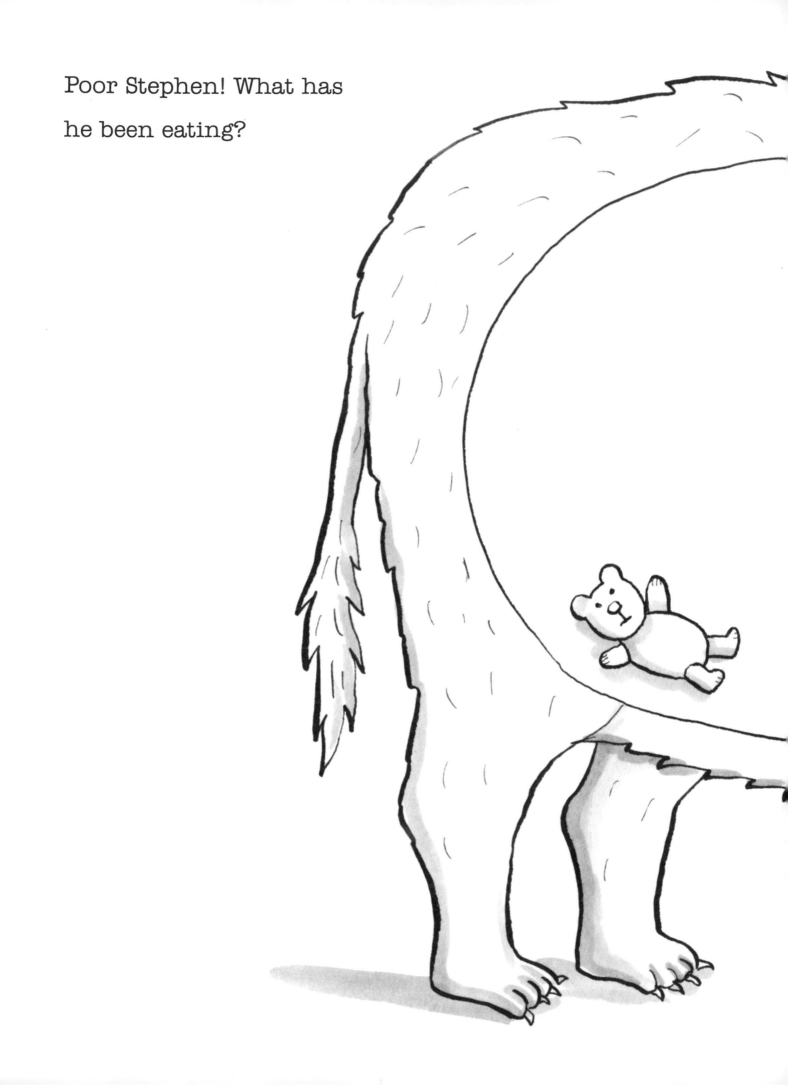

Axel Scheffler

Birds in frocks
and socks...

chris Riddell

followed by a   Bear in a Cheesey hat,
                               Bauble mittens,
                               Jingle bell coat
                                     and
                               Snuggly slippers...

                                         followed
                                         by ...

Create and colour creatures!

Kitty Crowther

These giraffes need some patterns.

Emma Carlisle

SPECIAL CREATURE DELIVERY!

DRAW A BABY CREATURE BEING CARRIED IN THE STORK'S CLOTH BUNDLE.

Nikki Dyson.

With thanks to all
of the brilliant artists below:

Adam Stower • Alex T. Smith • Alexis Deacon

Ami Shin • Axel Scheffler • Barbara Nascimbeni

Benjamin Chaud • Benji Davies • Birgitta Sif

Briony May Smith • Britta Teckentrup

Chris Riddell • David Mackintosh • David Roberts

Ekaterina Trukhan • Emily Gravett

Emily MacKenzie • Emma Carlisle • Jan Pieńkowski

Jean Jullien • Jim Field • Jools Bentley

Katherina Manolessou • Kazuno Kohara

Kitty Crowther • Lorna Scobie • Marta Altés

Matt Spink • Natalie Russell

Nikki Dyson • Poly Bernatene • Rebecca Patterson

Rilla • Rob Biddulph • Russell Ayto

Sara Ogilvie • Sarah McIntyre • Susanne Göhlich

Sven Nordqvist • Tim Hopgood • Tor Freeman

Yasmeen Ismail • Zehra Hicks

First published 2015 by Macmillan Children's Books, an imprint of Pan Macmillan. 20 New Wharf Road, London N1 9RR. Associated companies throughout the world. www.panmacmillan.com ISBN: 978-1-4472-9070-4. Copyright © Macmillan Publishers International Limited 2015. All illustrations copyright © the individual illustrators. The right of the individual illustrators to be identified as the illustrators of this work has been asserted by them in accordance with the Copyright, Designs and Patents Act 1988. All rights reserved. No part of this publication may be reproduced, stored in a retrieval system, or transmitted, in any form or by any means (electronic, mechanical, photocopying, recording or otherwise), without the prior written permission of the publisher. A CIP catalogue record for this book is available from the British Library. Printed in Italy. 9 8 7 6 5 4 3 2 1